#28

S0-CPT-025

70

NO
BOYS
ALLOWED

Other books by Susan Terris

NO
BOYS
ALLOWED

by Susan Terris

Illustrated by Richard Cuffari

Doubleday & Company, Inc., Garden City, New York

Library of Congress Cataloging in Publication Data

Terris, Susan.
  No boys allowed.

  SUMMARY: An eight-year-old boy with four sisters
is in need of boy's lib.
  [1. Brothers and sisters—Fiction] I. Cuffari,
  Richard, 1925-   illus. II. Title.
PZ7.T276No   [Fic]
ISBN 0-385-04887-4 Trade
     0-385-05749-0 Prebound
Library of Congress Catalog Card Number 74-23348

Printed in the United States of America

First Edition

For Ted, for Robert, and for Julia . . .
    because each of you knows what it's like to
    be the youngest. . . .

Tullius Cicero Sharp IV. My name. The most important thing about me. But no one calls me that. They call me Tad. Or little Tad because I'm eight and the youngest in my family.

My family. There's Dad and Ma. They're okay. I live with them in an apartment in San Francisco. But the rest of our place is full of sisters—four of them. So full of sisters that sometimes, like last Tuesday, I feel like a boy with five mothers.

8   Last Tuesday—March first—was Ma's birthday. My sisters all had presents, and I didn't have anything. And, because they were planning a surprise dinner for Ma, they started giving me orders the minute I got home from school.

"Do this," they said. "Do that."

My bossy sisters. No one bossed them. They were free. Old enough to go downtown or to the movies whenever they wanted. Old enough to have afterschool jobs. My liberated sisters. They talked a lot about growing up to be important and about having careers. Women's lib, they said.

Now I don't mind women's lib—only women's lip.

"Move this," they said. "Move that."

"What about me?" I asked. "Did you come see what kind of party *I* thought we should give? Did you take *me* along to buy presents for Ma? What about children's lib? Youngest child's lib? What about boys' lib?"

10　"Shut up," they said. "We're busy. Go out and play."

I went out all right. I grabbed my car-washing money and caught the number 3 Jackson bus downtown. Didn't tell anyone I was going. They would've said no—Ma and the sisters always think I'm too young to do things for myself.

Being downtown with money stuffed in my back pocket made me feel good. I wasn't in

12 any hurry because it was only four and no one would be looking for me until six, so I walked around for a long time trying to think what Ma might like for a present.

Then I found a creepy shop full of glass bottles and an old woman. There was a flower holder in the window that looked just about right. I had enough money, too—even if I did have to count out a lot of pennies to make it.

As soon as the woman put the flower thing

in a bag, I said, "Thanks," and hurried out of the shop. I was proud of my present. When I got home, I'd wrap it up and write a card that said, "Happy Birthday, from T. C. Sharp IV."

I was waiting at the bus stop when it hit me. No money. I'd spent it all—except for two pennies. So there I was by myself on a downtown corner with a present for Ma but no money for bus fare.

Well, I decided, I had feet. And I knew the

way home. Just about three miles straight out Jackson Street would do it. If I hurried, I'd get back before dark. Before Ma or the sisters knew I was gone.

So I started walking. When I got near the big church on Taylor Street, I saw a bunch of choirboys who might've given me bus money. But I didn't ask. I could make it home by myself. No problem at all.

A few blocks past the church, I came to a store full of clocks ticking off the time. "Five twenty-five," said a tall grandfather clock in the window. But when I squinted, I could see that some of the other clocks said "five thirty" and "five thirty-five." It *was* getting late, so I tried to walk faster.

I had never known there were so many hills along Jackson. They slowed me down but I kept going. Then on top of one hill where I stopped for breath, I saw some girls playing.

"Go away!" they yelled when they saw me coming. "No boys allowed!"

There was this tall one with a jump rope.
She said she was Anita and she was the boss around there.

Now I get that kind of stuff from my sisters. Too much of it. I was in a hurry but I still had time to tell off Anita.

"Don't give me that women's lib, women's lip stuff," I said. "Boys *are* allowed. If we have women's lib and girls' lib, we should have boys' lib! What about boys' lib?"

"What are you talking about, you block-head?" Anita asked.

I was just about to explain what I meant when her mother called her to come in for dinner. I turned away. Was it that late already?

Peanut butter. Hearing Anita's mother call her for dinner made my stomach rumble for a peanut-butter sandwich. And peanut butter made me think of the kitchen at home and of my family. Had they missed me? Were they worried?

20 "Keep walking," I told myself. "And forget about the peanut butter."

I tried counting steps to make the time pass. One hundred and eight for one block. One hundred and seven for another. But I couldn't stretch far enough to get there in one hundred and six.

Everything was fine until I got to Alta Park. It was cold and foggy there. No one was playing ball. No one was on the swings. The benches were all empty.

There was only me. And this lady. "You
should be home, boy," she said. "Look at the
time. It's six thirty-nine. Are you lost? Have
you run away? Does your momma know
where you are? How old are you? Seven?
Eight? You're too young to be out alone after
dark. Look—look there—the street lights just
went on. You don't see any other children
around, do you? If you were mine, I'd give
you a whipping for being out so late. Don't
you have any sense in that head of yours?"

She kept on talking and talking until I backed away and started to run. One minute I was fine, just making my way home. And the next, I was scared and running.

I was in such a hurry to get away that I stepped right out in front of a truck. Brakes screeched. Some man yelled at me. But I didn't stop.

Still running, I tried to think of all the things I'd ever been told about being alone. In my ear a mother-voice, sister-voice kept

whispering, "Don't talk to strangers."

Right. I'd been fine until I talked to that lady in Alta Park. Or until she'd talked to me . . .

Things around me were starting to look strange. Strange and shadowy. When I looked up from the sidewalk, I could see children's faces looking out of all the lighted windows. At least, I thought I saw them. They looked warm and safe while I was cold and alone, and the city was getting darker. And foggier.

All of a sudden, I seemed to be seeing faces everywhere. Mother faces. Sister faces. My face. My face about to cry. The face of a man in rags standing on the corner, flapping his arms. *Was* it a man? Or was it just a telephone pole full of half-torn-off posters?

I was seeing faces in windows. On buildings. All around me. Getting bigger. Closing in. What was happening to me? And where were my five mothers now?

Around me there were faces and inside my head a voice—the mother-voice, sister-voice. "Don't talk to strangers," it said. "Where are you? What are you doing? Why aren't you home for our birthday dinner? You're too young to be out alone at night. Don't talk to strangers."

"I'm okay—as okay as anyone in all of San Francisco!" I shouted at a stone lion.

A strange stone lion. He didn't answer. He just stared down at me until I shivered and turned away.

Then the stone lion made a noise—a wailing, whining noise. I looked back. But it wasn't the lion, only the sound made by a siren starting up somewhere nearby. A fire engine or a police-car siren. Someone was in danger. Someone was hurt or in trouble.

Listening to the siren made me feel weird. Weird and shivery. Was that a police car or a fire engine out looking for me?

I felt sick. My stomach was aching and I was holding the paper bag so tight I almost

cracked the flower thing I'd bought. It was very dark now and there were still more blocks to go.

"The street lights *should* help," I told myself, as I ran from one circle of light to another. But they didn't. There was too much darkness and fog in between.

I was getting closer, though. There ahead of me was the old Blaine place that had burned on Halloween. If I cut through that yard, I'd get home faster.